Penguins!

GENTOO PENGUINS

by Jody S. Rake

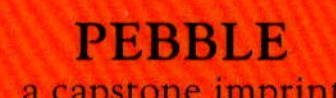

Pebble Plus is published by Pebble
1710 Roe Crest Drive, North Mankato, Minnesota 56003
www.mycapstone.com

Library of Congress Cataloging-in-Publication Data
Names: Rake, Jody Sullivan, author.
Title: Gentoo penguins / by Jody S. Rake.
Description: North Mankato, Minnesota : Capstone, an imprint of Pebble,
[2020] | Series: Pebble plus. Penguins! | Audience: Age 5-6. | Audience: K to Grade 3.
Identifiers: LCCN 2019008832 |
ISBN 9781977109361 (hardcover)
ISBN 9781977109422 (ebook PDF)
Subjects: LCSH: Gentoo penguin--Juvenile literature.
Classification: LCC QL696.S473 R356 2020 | DDC 598.47--dc23
LC record available at https://lccn.loc.gov/2019008832

Editorial Credits
Donald Lemke, editor; Ted Williams, designer; Kelly Garvin, media researcher;
Tori Abraham, production specialist

Photo Credits
Shutterstock: Alexey Seafarer, 17, 19, Amplion, 6, Brendan van Son, 13, Designus, 6, fieldwork, cover, 15, 21, Giedriius, 11, K Ireland, 9, Kyle Waters, 7, Stephen Lew, 1, Volodymyr Goinyk, 5

Design elements: Shutterstock/Rashad Ashur

Printed and bound in China.
1654

TABLE OF CONTENTS

The Penguin With EarMuffs 4
Island Penguins 8
Gentoo Nests and Chicks 12
Dangers to Gentoos. 20

Glossary .22
Read More 23
Internet Sites 23
Critical Thinking Questions 24
Index 24

THE PENGUIN WITH EARMUFFS

Gentoo penguins have black and white feathers. They have a white patch above their eyes and across their heads. Gentoos look like they're wearing earmuffs!

Gentoo penguins are the third-largest penguins. They are about as tall as a fire hydrant. Gentoos weigh up to 17.6 pounds (8 kilograms).

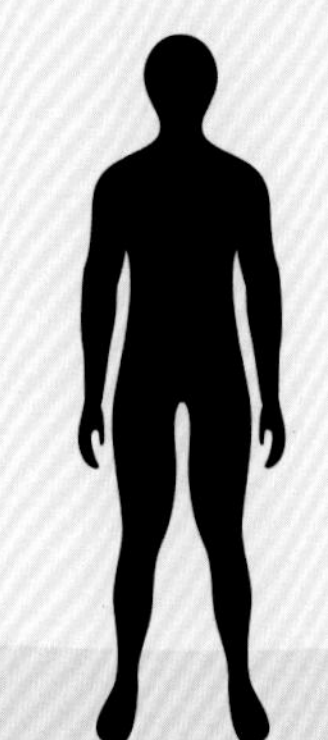

60 inches
(152 centimeters) tall.

30 inches
(76 centimeters) tall.

ISLAND PENGUINS

Gentoo penguins live on islands near Antarctica and South America. Gentoos live on rocky and grassy land away from ice. They live in large colonies.

Gentoo penguins are the fastest of all penguins. They flap their flippers to swim.

Gentoos hunt for food in the sea. They eat krill, fish, and squid.

GENTOO NESTS AND CHICKS

A father gentoo penguin gives a pebble to the mother. He points his beak to the sky and calls loudly. If she likes his gift, she makes a nest with him.

Gentoos build nests on the ground. They make a little hill of mud. The penguins line the nest with grass and pebbles. They use feathers and shells too.

A mother gentoo lays two eggs
about three days apart.
Both parents care for the eggs.
One parent keeps the eggs warm.
The other hunts for food.

Eggs hatch in about a month. The chicks are covered with warm, gray down. Soon the chicks will grow waterproof feathers. Then they can swim and hunt.

DANGERS TO GENTOOS

Gentoo penguins have many predators. Killer whales, leopard seals, and sea lions hunt gentoos. Gentoos live about 15 to 20 years.

GLOSSARY

beak—the hard, front part of the mouth of birds

colony—a large group of the same kind of animal living together

down—the soft, fluffy feathers of a baby bird

feather—one of the light, fluffy parts that cover a bird's body

flipper—one of the long, flat upper limbs of a penguin; flippers help penguins swim.

hatch—to break out of an egg

krill—small, shrimp-like animal

predator—an animal that hunts other animals for food

waterproof—not allowing water to soak through

READ MORE

Hall, Margaret. *Penguins and Their Chicks: A 4D Book.* Animal Offspring. North Mankato, Minn.: Capstone Press, 2018.

Salomon, David. *Penguins!* Step Into Reading. New York: Random House, 2017.

Williams, Kathryn. *Hello, Penguin!* National Geographic Kids. Washington, D.C.: National Geographic, 2017.

INTERNET SITES

Kiddle: Gentoo Penguin Facts
https://kids.kiddle.co/Gentoo_penguin

PenguinWorld
http://www.penguinworld.com/types/gentoo.html

KidZone: Penguins
https://www.kidzone.ws/animals/penguins/

CRITICAL THINKING QUESTIONS

1. What special markings do gentoo penguins have that are different from other penguins?
2. Where do Gentoo penguins live?
3. When can a Gentoo chick begin to swim and hunt?

INDEX

Antarctica, 8
beaks, 12
chicks, 18
colonies, 8
eggs, 16, 18
feathers, 4, 14, 18
flippers, 10
hunting, 10, 16, 18, 20
islands, 8
nests, 12, 14
pebbles, 12, 14
predators, 20
South America, 8
swimming, 10, 18
weight, 6